Earth Energy Healing-
THE GRIDWORKER'S FIELD GUIDE

Companion workbook to
A Portal to Earth Energy

by: Kenzie Ann Rhodess
Doctor of Divinity

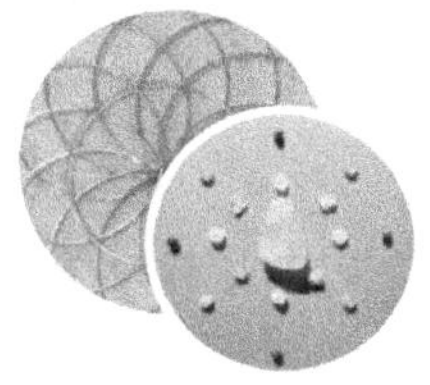

A Portal to Earth Energy The Path of the Gridworker
Published by Azuray Productions;
Hampden County on Massachusetts
Copyright © 2023 by Kenzie Rhodes

www.crystalgridearthenergyhealing.com

Azuray
Productions

Table of Contents

Introduction to the Workbook.................................4
Chapter One-Start Where you Are........................ 5
Chapter Two-Foundations: The Mental...................12
Chapter Three- Foundations: Spiritual Hygiene... 15
Chapter Four-Tools: The Practitioner.. 23
Chapter Five-Tools: The Crystal Grid.....................27
Chapter Six-Tools: Planning....................................35
Chapter Seven-Timing & Location...........................39
Chapter Eight Execution:Physical Crystal Grids...49
Chapter Nine-Remote Gridwork Missions...............63
A Final Word on Cold False-Light..........................113

Introduction

A Portal to Earth Energy, The Path of the Gridworker was not only written to call the reader's attention to the similarities between the Divine blueprint of the human and of Earth, but also to serve as a launchpad for gridwork exploration and spiritual development. The first porton of the workbook is conceptual and big picture; it is designed to assist with reflection, which turns the lens inward. The second portion is practical and concrete, focusing on tools and practices. The last portion is about action. Some readers may be more interested in getting directly into the tools, and the action steps, while others may want to expand the scope of their entire spiritual journey through this work. Take what you can use and leave the rest behind.

The path of the gridworker is the path of a healer, and is as individual as the many people who are recognizing that their mission here on Earth is healing in one form or another.

This workbook is meant to assist you in clarifying your intentions in this work, and to help you to track your spiritual evolution. It is also meant to provide some organizational structure to help you figure out your own process as you learn what works for you. Additional space has been provided to journal and reflect upon your insights and experiences as you move through the journey. As always, I welcome your ideas and input and invite you to visit my website at www.crystalgridearthenergyhealing.com or email me at kayazuray@yahoo.com

It can be used in conjunction with the book (link to author page https://www.amazon.com/author/kenzierhodes-earthenergyhealer), or as a stand-alone guide.

Chapter One - Start Where you Are
"He who knows others is wise; he who knows himself is enlightened"
- Lao Tsu

Deep spiritual work requires the integration of different levels of perception. There are two perceptual orientations along the pendulum swing; recognition of the forest, and recognition of the trees. You must flow with both. This falls within the Universal, Cosmic Law of Rhythm; when you master both perceptions and integrate them into unity, you are able to begin activating the other higher Laws. The inverted systems; frequency fences, have trapped humanity in low-frequency, slavery consciousness that plays out in mainstream reality (zeitgeist) by a hijacking of this Law within education, religion, science, medicine and government. Reductionist, sum-of-the-parts philosophies that are designed to train the brain to look with tunnel vision into silos have rendered much of humanity incapable of accessing higher perceptory awarenesses. The move away from generalizion (big-picture thinking, which is the ability to connect dots and see patterns) into specialization (detail-oriented thinking, which is the essence of reductionism and disconnection from the whole) has put people into mental boxes.

What does your comfort zone look like? You may not have reflected on this question before, so spend some time considering your past practices and your own orientation. Is it natural....or has it been influenced over the years? What influences have guided this in your life?

____

____

____

____

____

____

____

____

____

____

____

List examples of times when you employed very detail-oriented thinking....and times of big-picture thinking. Where do you currently land with regard to your comfort level using both of these orientations?

____

____

____

____

____

____

____

____

____

____

____

____

What are some ways that you can consciously work to strengthen your abilities to see the world from a different lens than that which you are most comfortable using?

____
____
____
____
____
____
____
____
____
____
____

Gridworking is both a spiritual discipline and a concrete practice. The journey depends entirely upon the intentions and goals of the practitioner. Take a moment to reflect upon where you are at this time, and think about how gridworking applies to your particular journey. This chapter will help you to begin organizing your thoughts and intentions as you start this work. Think also about your own personal connection to Earth, and ways that this is expressed in your life. Maybe you love to garden and grow plants. Maybe you have always appreciated rocks and crystals. Maybe it is a deep connection to the woods, and to Nature. All of these are examples of how Earth affinity is recognized.

What is it about gridworking that most appeals to you?

____
____
____
____
____
____
____

How did you discover Earth Energy and gridworking? Did you have signs or synchronicities that drew you to this path?

____
____
____
____
____
____
____
____
____
____
____
____

Now take a moment to clarify your intentions in gridworking as a spiritual discipline, and/or a practice. Overall (big picture), what do you hope to accomplish, both in the short term, and the long term?

____
____
____
____
____
____
____
____

What are the challenges, if any, that you face in doing this work? How will you overcome them?

____
____
____
____
____
____

What qualities, gifts and skills do you possess that you feel will be most helpful in gridworking? How will you apply them to the work?

____
____
____
____
____
____

List the future gridworking projects you would like to accomplish as you are turning over the page to a brand new chapter. As you move along and come up with new ideas, add them.

____

____

____

____

____

____

____

____

____

____

____

____

____

____

____

Reflections and Insights:

____

____

____

____

____

____

____

Reflections and Insights (Continued)...

Chapter Two - Foundations: The Mental
"The Universe is Mental" - The Kybalion

The first, most fundamental principal of Nature is that all reality is a mental expression of Divine Source. which is Unknowable. It is Spirit. This is a baseline for all work of a spiritual nature. This is the wellspring from which oceans, rivers and streams are birthed, and mastery of this principle serves as the foundation for all important work. The quality of that which you manifest is dependent upon the quality and strength of your foundation. The purpose of this chapter is preparatory, to help you stretch your mind muscles.

Consider different spiritual philosophies and practices that you are familiar with; those which resonate with you, and those which do not. What are their foundational principles?

____

____

____

____

____

____

____

____

____

____

____

How do these foundational principles relate to the recognition that Spirit is Unknowable? (an example is to consider "The Tao that can be spoken is not the Tao" - Tao Te Ching)

____

____

____

____

____

____

____

____

____

____

____

____

____

____

____

____

Reflections and Insights:

____

____

____

____

____

____

____

Reflections and Insights (Continued)...

CHAPTER THREE - FOUNDATIONS: SPIRITUAL HYGIENE

Spiritual hygiene consists of those foundational practices that keep your energy field clear of and protected from all blockages and attachments; sovereign. The practice of spiritual hygiene organically increases baseline consciousness levels because this is the natural result of a vessel that is freed from the physical density that these blockages cause.

Spiritual hygiene is not only energetic work, it also also highly physical. The physical body is intimately connected to the material world. It is the Anchor for the Spirit, through which manifestation occurs. The physical body is absolutely essential to any true spiritual practice, and all too often, its importance is completely dismissed by mainstream spiritual teachers and gurus. A little known truth is that people can spend endless hours in meditation and mental exercises and find that only short-lived positive changes happen in their lives because they neglect this most essential, fundamental concept. Do not make that mistake, and take with a grain of salt the teachings of anyone who does not establish this truth as a priority in their work.

Take a moment to consider your current spiritual practices in context to Spiritual Hygiene. How does your existing level of spiritual hygiene add to....or distract from your personal Sovereignty at this time?

____
____
____
____
____
____

A Portal to Earth Energy, the Path of the Gridworker presents some energy healing practices that address the clearing and cleansing aspect of spiritual hygiene by removing energetic blockages, implants and entity attachments. There also are many, many other methods, and more are coming into the collective consciousness every day.

What energy healing practices/processes are you currently exploring, and how have you used them in the past? What changes have you noticed in your spiritual awareness as a result of energy healing? If you have not explored energy healing, how might you benefit to do so?

____

____

____

____

____

____

____

____

Now think of energy healing as it relates to Earth. How could the practices that you utilize for your own spiritual hygiene potentially apply to her?

____

____

____

____

____

____

____

Energy clearing and cleansing affects both the energy bodies and the physical body; physical cleansing and clearing effects both the physical body and the energy bodies. For the greatest result, they must be used in conjunction to effect the entire template. In the material world, the essential components of this practice are detoxification and parasite removal, and the elimination of chemical exposures from dietary and environmental sources.

What physical practices/processes are you currently exploring, and how have you used them in the past? What changes have you noticed in your spiritual awareness as a result of these practices? If you have not explored these concepts, what are your barriers?

Now, again relate these processes to Earth. What ways can you personally effect positive change for her? (This is more to help you be aware of your role, and the need to be conscious in context of your own habits. Consider not just your immediate environment, but also the Commons.)

The next level of spiritual hygiene is consumption, both physical and energetic, and it relates to quantity as well as quality. The old saying "garbage in...garbage out" applies! As the goal is to have the purest vessel possible, it is essential to recognize that vital life force requires proper nutrition, hydration, and balance in consumption.

What are your consumption habits? Consider all the different sources, including water intake. What are their effects on how you feel, physically, emotionally and spiritually? How can you improve upon this?

____
____
____
____
____
____
____
____

Now, consider Earth with regard to what she is consuming through the actions and intentions of the human population. There are actual physical manifestations in certain areas that are a direct reflection of the quality of life of her inhabitants. What are some of your observations?

____
____
____
____
____
____

The next, all-important component of spiritual hygiene after clearing, cleansing is infusing the template with nutrition; physical nutrition and emotional and spiritual nutrition. This also relates to consumption, and whether what is being consumed is feeding the body and soul, or stealing vital life force from them.

What are your current habits with regard to nutrition? Are there any changes that you can make that will improve this area?

____
____
____
____
____
____
____
____

Now, again relate this question to Earth; what gives essential nutrients to her, and how can you personally take action to help this?

____
____
____
____
____
____
____
____

Cultivating a regular practice of grounding, shielding and protecting your Energy Field is the final, essential cornerstone of good spiritual hygiene. These topics, and instructions for different practices are discussed at length in *A Portal to Earth Energy*, as well as in numerous books and literature available to students on a spiritual path.

Do you consistently practice techniques to physically ground yourself to Earth every day, and to energetically shield and protect your energy bodies? What are your techniques, and what, if any, improvements are needed to fully commit to this important intention?

____
____
____
____
____
____
____

As you practice and learn by doing, what changes are you noticing with regard to the way that you feel in your body and in your Spirit?

____
____
____
____
____
____
____

The more that you explore these different levels of a healthy foundation, the more that you are probably realizing how interconnected they really are, which is a validation of the truth behind these practices. Self-reflection is an essential part of spiritual growth; it gives confirmation of your own gnosis and builds discernment.

None of these practices are a one-and-done; they must be done regularly, with continous and ongoing attention. Grounding, shielding and protection must be done every day, as well as paying attention to consumption. Detoxing and parasite removal must be done every few months. Simply by being conscious of all these things, you will find yourself growing and expanding, and your consciousness level will slowly rise.

Reflections and Insights:

____
____
____
____
____
____
____
____
____
____
____
____
____

Reflections and Insights (Continued)...

CHAPTER FOUR - Tools: the Practitioner
"Intuition is the number one tool in the toolbox"- Matthew Mellon

Preparation and organization of tools are actions that help to move manifestation from the non-corporeal realms into the physical, material realm. Just as the physical human body is the anchor that contains the Soul Spirit, Earth is the anchor that contains her Soul Spirit; her consciousness. Tools are a bridge to manifestation through those anchors into the material world, and they hold the consciousness of the intentions of the work in place. This in turn causes an energetic reverberation that echoes through all the levels of the energy body. While gridworking can certainly be done with just two feet and a focused intention, the use of tools is very powerful and helpful in the practice.

Every gridworker is an energy healer, and will eventually determine his or her own preferential tools for the work. *A Portal to Earth Energy* discusses some of the different energy healing modalities which utilize tools keyed to sound frequency and light, and there are also other tools that different practitioners use in their personal disciplines. Many of them are combined very effectively into a unique style of healing that works very well for each individual practitioner.

The similarities between the human blueprint and the Earth's blueprint are quite remarkable. as are the implications for affecting change. You are strongly encouraged to begin exploring ways that you can take your existing practices for healing and begin experimenting on ways to apply them intentionally to Earth healing.

What special tool do you plan to use (or currently do use) to focus and direct your intention in order to activate your grids, such as a personal Vogel cut crystal or another type of rod or wand? This is an essential tool that every gridworker should have.

____
____
____
____
____

What supplemental tools (such as pendulum, dowsing rods, or clearing and smudging wand) could you use in addition to the wand?

____
____
____
____
____
____
____
____

What is it about these items that resonates with you? What steps can you take to increase your connection to your personal tools, and enhance the resonance in get greater results in gridwork?

____
____
____
____
____

What other methods have you considered adding to your gridwork toolbox? Will you bring in sound frequencies, mudras, or light codes, or some other tool of energy healing? List the possibilities that you want to explore.

____

____

____

____

____

____

____

____

____

____

What challenges (if any) do you face in implementing these ideas, and what must you do to overcome them? (This could include additional study, difficulty acquiring necessary items, et al).

____

____

____

____

____

____

____

____

Reflections and Insights...

CHAPTER FIVE - Tools: the Crystal Grid

In addition to the skills and personal tools brought forward by the practitioner, physical gridwork in the material realm should also include an intentional pattern, and physical anchors. Crystals, because they are of Earth and hold stable and enduring consciousness frequencies, are instrumental to this purpose. Familiarity with geometric patterns or runes, depending upon individual preference, is also very helpful.

If you haven't used crystals before, you can find numerous sources of information in books and internet websites that list the characteristics and spiritual meaning of different crystals. The general rule of thumb is that the color of the crystal reflects its correspondence to certain qualities that resonate with levels of consciousness....and relate to a chakra. Rose quartz, for instance, is pink in color and it carries the consciousness of the heart chakra; love, compassion, healing, acceptance. Tiger eye has golds, browns, reds and oranges in it, and it carries the consciousness of the root and the sacral chakras; grounding, protection, security, connection to family. The same principles apply to all crystals.

When laying crystal grids in specific patterns out in Nature, and even in a special, undisturbed place inside the home, you will want to be very intentional. At the center of the pattern will be a carefully-chosen Centering Stone. This stone should contain the energies and consciousness of whatever goal you have for the work. It should address the needs of the location or of a particular situation that you desire to manifest. The Centering Stone is the focal point, radiating intention and crystal consciousness outward energetically.

An example of this would be an amethyst pyramid that your grandmother gave to you with the intention of bringing you healing and comfort during a time when you were young and had felt like you had lost your way, disconnected from Source. The shape and the crystal itself, as well as the powerful energies of the loving and protective bond between you and your grandmother are all contained within this single stone, which vibrates to the crown chakra and is connected to Divine Source consciousness. This would make a powerful Centering Stone for a crystal grid in the front yard of your home.

Take a moment and think of some crystals that you or members of your family or friends have that are special. What are the energies of consciousness that are contained within these crystals? How might these be used intentially in a grid for that person to manifest change, or as an amplification?

____
____
____
____
____
____
____
____
____
____

Now flip the lens and think about a challenging or difficult situation that you or someone you care about has gone through. What consciousness frequencies do you feel would be most needed to heal, strengthen or correct the challenge? Which crystal contains the most powerful and concentrated energy for this situation?

____
____
____
____
____
____
____
____
____
____
____

This exercise will help you to begin bringing in focus for your specific intentions. A crystal grid pattern can be very simple, or it can be very complicated, but when there is a very specific purpose for the work, it is necessary to be highly focused. Your results will be much stronger if you use the right tool for the particular job at hand, rather than taking a more broad-spectrum approach. Always be intentional and focused when you are selecting your Centering Stone. Remember, also that it is not necessary to use a stone that is personal and relevant for an individual every time, but sometimes that is the best stone for the job.

Additional crystals bring in supplemental energies to the Centering Stone of a crystal grid, which can add support and also serve as an amplifier. An example of this for the amethyst pyramid crystal grid referenced above would be a layer of blue topaz, which resonates with peace, calming, spiritual connection and truth; all of which are needed when someone feels lost in the wilderness and is going through a dark night of the soul. Another layer of Pure quartz crystals will bring in the energies of alignment and Source connection, and are a powerful amplifier for the crystal grid.

In the situation that you've just reflected upon, what additional crystals would you bring into the grid to add support, and to magnify the overall intentions? List some of the energies, and which crystals embody them.

____
____
____
____
____
____
____
____
____
____
____
____
____

The final layer of a typical crystal grid can be placed around the parameter. When you are placing a permanent crystal grid in the Earth, it is very helpful to place outer crystal points in the four cardinal directions (or the eight compass point directions, or even twelve locations) to ring the crystal grid out on the land. The same principles apply when you are decided which crystals to use; this is a good place to add black tourmaline or another highly protective stone, alongside an aventurine chip, (a good luck stone), or an apatite stone (the stone of manifestation).

The key is balance; whether it is one cystal or several, make sure that each outer point is the same. The crystal grid should always be balanced and have organic symmetry. As mentioned earlier, a crystal grid can be complicated or it can be as simple as a Centering Stone and four outer crystals placed in the North, South, East and West. It is all about the preference and the intuition of the gridworker.

What crystals come to mind that would serve as the finishing touch on your grid in this exercise and why?. In what pattern would you place them?

____
____
____
____
____
____
____

As you begin practicing with crystals, you will find it helpful to create a toolbox and keep everything organized. A fishing tackle box or another type of box with drawers and pockets serves this purpose very well. You can keep your crystal wand, examples of runes and geometric designs, copper wire, pencils and paper, and crystals of different sizes all in one place. Keep track of the details of your work, and your observations during spiritual exploration and gridwork practice.

What are the essentials that you will need for your individual toolbox?

____
____
____
____
____
____
____
____

Geometry is the language of the Universe, and geometric shapes are used as the container for crystal gridworking. Explore the spiritual significance and frequency of some of the different patterns. Runes are also very powerful, especially when they speak the language of the practitioner's ancestors. Familiarize yourself with patterns of sacred geometry, runes, hieroglyphs and other symbols that resonate with you, either in books or in internet searches, and think about the ways that they can be incorporated into gridworking.

What patterns resonate with you? Can you relate certain shapes with crystal grids that you would like to try? What are the meanings and the intentions contained within these patterns?

____

____

____

____

____

____

____

____

Reflections and Insights...

____

____

____

____

____

____

____

____

____

____

____

____

____

Reflections and Insights...

CHAPTER SIX - TOOLS - Planning

As you plan your gridworking mission, you will need to decide what the structure will look like. The Earth's grid template follows specific patterns; organic patterns such as ley lines, dragon lines, star gates, and areas of intersecting energies expressed organically in nodes and vortices, and inorganically in wormholes, inversions, harvesting-sites and implant technologies. *A Portal to Earth Energy* contains much information regarding this, and there are also numerous other sources available for the serious student.

From a big-picture perspective, what physical location are you most interested in targeting first for gridwork, and why?

____

____

____

____

____

When considering the energies of a particular location, it is very helpful to get a visual of the area. This can be as simple as taking a map, and drawing/labelling specific places on the map which carry a particular frequency, either benevolent or malevolent, and uncovering the pattern of connection between them. You will very often find that within an area that is holding a particularly dense consciousness, implant technologies have been built or placed over ancient sites of concentrated Earth Energy, siphoning the organic life force from the site while at the same time locking down the inhabitants who inhabit these areas. An example is the City of Detroit, Michigan; this is a well-known location of high crime, poverty, human suffering and misery for the current population, yet once there are many sacred sites that were revered by the Native population who lived there in harmony with Nature and each other before our current societal time. This area falls upon an ancient ley line that is very connected to indigenous Native American tribal medicine. There are numerous implant technologies that have been strategically placed to siphon away the organic energy, and to run artificial frequencies throughout the whole area. The malevolent effects of this can be seen reflected in the consciousness of the population residing there. This effect is an example of the Cosmic Law of Correspondence; As Above, So Below...As Within, As Without. That which is expressed in the material realm as a physical manifestation is the direct result of what is going on in the unseen realms operating behind them. Earth Energy is a potent cause-point.

With this principle in mind, think about the energy of your immediate location; your home/neighborhood. What is the general level of consciousness around you, and in context to the Earth Energies of your area, what could be contributing to this?

____
____
____
____
____
____
____
____

On a broader scale, what is the energetic signature of the overall consciousness within the population throughout your region? What is influencing this, either to the positive or the negative?

____

Map out some visual representations of these two examples and see what patterns you detect. Play with latitude and longitude to see if you can relate anything to an Earth Energy line. What are your observations?

Does this exercise give you any insight into what might be going in in other locations across the Earth, more distant than your immediate surroundings? Could there be a particular cause point somewhere far away? Reflecting on this will help you to discern levels of power with regard to Earth Energy and also of inversion technologies.

Reflections and Insights...

CHAPTER SEVEN - Timing & location

Where and when will you grid? Obviously, climate and accessibility are important considerations when developing plans to go out into Nature and do physical gridwork to affect whole areas. Gridworking can also be done remotely in a group, or privately through meditation and ritual, and the later chapter on Remote Gridworking will provide some structure for that work, as well as several templates that you can use to lay out your plans for remote gridwork missions. In this chapter, we will cover permanent crystal grids and temporary grids inside the home.

Astrological and numerological correspondences are very helpful for gridwork planning. The language of the Universe is mathematical; geometry is its expression. There is a reason why the Quadrivium quantifies reality within the context of just four principles; arithmetic, geometry, astronomy and music. Astrology and numerology are the logos of astronomy and arithmetic; this is the integration (second pillar of the Trivium) of knowledge (first pillar of the Trivium) within the template of these two fundamental sciences. The third pillar of the Trivium is wisdom, which is the alchemy that results from integrating deep exploration and understanding of the first two pillars.

This is a very big-picture overview, and many who are new to spirituality will find it confusing. Stick with it, mull it over, and perhaps do a little bit of further independent study. At the end of the day; realize that there are universal forces at play which do contain archetypal energies that have real time effects on the material world. Indigenous cultures of the past were far more aware of them than many existing in the Source-disconnected societies of today.

Consider your current level of awareness of universal energies in context of how they relate to manifestation in the physical world. What system or philosophy resonates with you? Is it Numerology? Vedic or Western Astrology? Tarot? Pure elemental energy (the Path of Four)? Something else? *

____
____
____
____
____
____
____
____

After you recognize where you are, think of how you can apply this to the gridworking project that you previously identified. What are the universal influences that would the most beneficial to add to your work, and how can you plan for this?

____
____
____
____
____
____
____
____
____
____

Consider the local, regional or universal influences that will be coming into play over the coming weeks and months. What are the energetic essences that are being highlighted in the upcoming holidays, celebrations, and other events?

____
____
____
____
____
____
____
____

This chapter is about growing your awareness of patterns with the goal of relating them to intentional work. Traditions, celebrations and holidays are rooted in a recognition of ritual....which is at its core actual Ceremonial Magic. All cultures, and all religions have this at their core. What are some examples that you can think of that reflect this?

____
____
____
____
____
____
____
____

Why do you suppose that some traditional religions, rather than recognizing the principles of Ceremonial Magic within their practice, instead use language that actively attempts to instil fear in people over the very idea of it?

____
____
____
____
____
____
____
____

In going through the exercises in this course, what insights have come to you? Have you noticed any shifts in your perceptions?

____
____
____
____
____
____
____
____

On the following pages, make a list of the gridwork missions that you are considering. Tie them into the energetic influences that would be beneficial to maximize your results.

Mission: ____
   Goal: ____
Method: On-location grid: _____ Quantum grid: _______ Remote: _____
Projected Timeline: ______________________________________
  Why? (influences):

____

____

Mission: ____
 Goal: ____
Method: On-location grid: _____ Quantum grid: _______ Remote: _____
Projected Timeline: ______________________________________
 Why? (influences):

____

____

Mission: ____
 Goal: ____

Method: On-location grid: _____ Quantum grid: _______ Remote: _____
Projected Timeline: ______________________________________
 Why? (influences):

____

____

Mission: ____
 Goal: ____
Method: On-location grid: _____ Quantum grid: _______ Remote: _____
Projected Timeline: ______________________________________
 Why? (influences):

____

____

Mission: ____
   Goal: ____
Method: On-location grid: _____ Quantum grid: _________ Remote: _____
Projected Timeline: ____
   Why? (influences):

____

____

Mission: ____
   Goal: ____
Method: On-location grid: _____ Quantum grid: _________ Remote: _____
Projected Timeline: ____
   Why? (influences):

____

____

Mission: ____
   Goal: ____

Method: On-location grid: _____ Quantum grid: _________ Remote: _____
Projected Timeline: ____
   Why? (influences):

____

____

Mission: ____
   Goal: ____
Method: On-location grid: _____ Quantum grid: _________ Remote: _____
Projected Timeline: ____
   Why? (influences):

____

____

Mission: ____

   Goal: ____

Method: On-location grid: _____ Quantum grid: ________ Remote: _____

Projected Timeline: ____

   Why? (influences):

____

____

Mission: ____

   Goal: ____

Method: On-location grid: _____ Quantum grid: ________ Remote: _____

Projected Timeline: ____

   Why? (influences):

____

____

Mission: ____

   Goal: ____

Method: On-location grid: _____ Quantum grid: ________ Remote: _____

Projected Timeline: ____

   Why? (influences):

____

____

Mission: ____

   Goal: ____

Method: On-location grid: _____ Quantum grid: ________ Remote: _____

Projected Timeline: ____

   Why? (influences):

____

____

Mission: ____
    Goal: ____
Method: On-location grid: _____ Quantum grid: ________ Remote: _____
Projected Timeline: ____
    Why? (influences):

____

____

Mission: ____
 Goal: ____
Method: On-location grid: _____ Quantum grid: ________ Remote: _____
Projected Timeline: ____
 Why? (influences):

____

____

Mission: ____
 Goal: ____

Method: On-location grid: _____ Quantum grid: ________ Remote: _____
Projected Timeline: ____
 Why? (influences):

____

____

Mission: ____
 Goal: ____
Method: On-location grid: _____ Quantum grid: ________ Remote: _____
Projected Timeline: ____
 Why? (influences):

____

____

*There are many different practices and schools of thought, all of which are built upon mathematical and geometric foundational principles. Understanding of this is important for the deepest spiritual work, and should be the goal of every serious student of spirituality. A good place to start is the Trivium, the Quadrivium, the Cosmic, Natural Laws (or Principles) and Vortex Mathematics.

Insights and Reflections

____
____
____
____
____
____
____
____
____
____
____
____
____
____
____
____
____
____

Reflections and Insights...

CHAPTER EIGHT - Execution - physical crystal grids
"The path to success is ... massive, determined actions" - Tony Robbins

Now that you have done the preliminary work and gathered your tools, it is time to apply them. This chapter is about physical crystal grids, either outside in Nature, or in an undisturbed space indoors.

Step One: Determine your site

Step Two: Gather your tools; crystals, pattern, and accessories as well as your own practitioner tools

Step Three: On-location

Step Four: Charge your wand/state your intentions and ask for Divine assistance, and assistance from Earth

Step Five: Place your grid pattern, charging and programming the crystals with your intentions as you place them

Step Six: Charge completed grid

Step Seven: Visualize results & give thanks

This is the basic process. If you are going to an external location, you may wish to include other people to add their shared intentions to the work. When you arrive at your site, it might be helpful to lay out the grid pattern preliminarily and to visualize all the crystals working together to manifest the results before you take them and begin planting them in the Earth. Sometimes, when dealing with crowded locations where you don't really want to attract the attention of curious onlookers, it makes sense to do a bit of the energetic work to really charge and program the crystals before you actually place them into the Earth, or on the pattern board in your home that you have set aside for a temporary crystal grid. Gridworking is experiential, and intention is key.

Crystal Grid Itinerary

Location: _______________________________________

Participants: ____________________________________

Date/Time: ______________________________________

Intention Statement: _____________________________

____

Chosen Pattern:

Centering Stone/meaning: _________________________
First layer/meaning: _____________________________
Second layer/meaning: ____________________________
Third layer/meaning: _____________________________
Fourth layer/meaning: ____________________________

Parameter stones/meaning: ________________________

Additional accessories: __________________________
Healing modalities to include: ___________________
____
____
Observations/Signs:

____
____
____
____
____
____
____

Crystal Grid Itinerary

Location: ____

Participants: ____

Date/Time: ____

Intention Statement: ________________________________

____

Chosen Pattern:

Centering Stone/meaning: ____________________________

First layer/meaning: _________________________________

Second layer/meaning: _______________________________

Third layer/meaning: ________________________________

 Fourth layer/meaning: _______________________________

Parameter stones/meaning: ___________________________

Additional accessories: ______________________________

Healing modalities to include: _______________________

____

____

Observations/Signs:

____

____

____

____

____

____

____

Crystal Grid Itinerary

Location: _______________________________________

Participants: _____________________________________

Date/Time: ______________________________________

Intention Statement: ______________________________

____

Chosen Pattern:

Centering Stone/meaning: ___________________________

First layer/meaning: ______________________________

Second layer/meaning: _____________________________

Third layer/meaning: ______________________________

Fourth layer/meaning: _____________________________

Parameter stones/meaning: __________________________

Additional accessories: ____________________________

Healing modalities to include: _______________________

____

____

Observations/Signs:

____

____

____

____

____

____

____

Crystal Grid Itinerary

Location: _______________________________________

Participants: _______________________________________

Date/Time: _______________________________________

Intention Statement: _______________________________

____

Chosen Pattern:

Centering Stone/meaning: _______________________________

First layer/meaning: _______________________________

Second layer/meaning: _______________________________

Third layer/meaning: _______________________________

Fourth layer/meaning: _______________________________

Parameter stones/meaning: _______________________________

Additional accessories: _______________________________

Healing modalities to include: _______________________________

____

____

Observations/Signs:

____

____

____

____

____

____

____

Crystal Grid Itinerary

Location: ____

Participants: ____

Date/Time: ____

Intention Statement: ____________________________________

____

Chosen Pattern:

Centering Stone/meaning: ________________________________

First layer/meaning: ____________________________________

Second layer/meaning: ___________________________________

Third layer/meaning: ____________________________________

Fourth layer/meaning: ___________________________________

Parameter stones/meaning: _______________________________

Additional accessories: _________________________________

Healing modalities to include: __________________________

____

____

Observations/Signs:

____

____

____

____

____

____

____

Crystal Grid Itinerary

Location: ____

Participants: ____________________________________

Date/Time: ______________________________________

Intention Statement: ____________________________

____

Chosen Pattern:

Centering Stone/meaning: _______________________________

First layer/meaning: ___________________________________

Second layer/meaning: _________________________________

Third layer/meaning: __________________________________

Fourth layer/meaning: _________________________________

Parameter stones/meaning: ____________________________

Additional accessories: _______________________________

Healing modalities to include: ________________________

____

____

Observations/Signs:

____

____

____

____

____

____

____

Crystal Grid Itinerary

Location: ____

Participants: _______________________________________

Date/Time: ____

Intention Statement: _______________________________

____

Chosen Pattern:

Centering Stone/meaning: ___________________________

First layer/meaning: ________________________________

Second layer/meaning: ______________________________

Third layer/meaning: _______________________________

Fourth layer/meaning: ______________________________

Parameter stones/meaning: __________________________

Additional accessories: _____________________________

Healing modalities to include: ______________________

____

____

Observations/Signs:

____

____

____

____

____

____

____

Crystal Grid Itinerary

Location: ____

Participants: ____

Date/Time: ____

Intention Statement: ___________________________________

____

Chosen Pattern:

Centering Stone/meaning: ___________________________________

First layer/meaning: ___________________________________

Second layer/meaning: ___________________________________

Third layer/meaning: ___________________________________

Fourth layer/meaning: ___________________________________

Parameter stones/meaning: ___________________________________

Additional accessories: ___________________________________

Healing modalities to include: ___________________________________

____

____

Observations/Signs:

____

____

____

____

____

____

____

Crystal Grid Itinerary

Location: ___________________________________

Participants: ___________________________________

Date/Time: ___________________________________

Intention Statement: ___________________________________

____

Chosen Pattern:

Centering Stone/meaning: ___________________________________

First layer/meaning: ___________________________________

Second layer/meaning: ___________________________________

Third layer/meaning: ___________________________________

 Fourth layer/meaning: ___________________________________

Parameter stones/meaning: ___________________________________

Additional accessories: ___________________________________

Healing modalities to include: ___________________________________

____

____

Observations/Signs:

____

____

____

____

____

____

____

Crystal Grid Itinerary

Location: _______________________________________

Participants: _______________________________________

Date/Time: _______________________________________

Intention Statement: _______________________________

____

Chosen Pattern:

Centering Stone/meaning: _______________________________

First layer/meaning: _______________________________

Second layer/meaning: _______________________________

Third layer/meaning: _______________________________

 Fourth layer/meaning: _______________________________

Parameter stones/meaning: _______________________________

Additional accessories: _______________________________

Healing modalities to include: _______________________________

____

____

Observations/Signs:

____

____

____

____

____

____

____

Crystal Grid Itinerary

Location: ___________________________________

Participants: ___________________________________

Date/Time: ___________________________________

Intention Statement: ___________________________________

____

Chosen Pattern:

Centering Stone/meaning: ___________________________________

First layer/meaning: ___________________________________

Second layer/meaning: ___________________________________

Third layer/meaning: ___________________________________

Fourth layer/meaning: ___________________________________

Parameter stones/meaning: ___________________________________

Additional accessories: ___________________________________

Healing modalities to include: ___________________________________

____

____

Observations/Signs:

____

____

____

____

____

____

____

Crystal Grid Itinerary

Location: _______________________________________

Participants: _____________________________________

Date/Time: _______________________________________

Intention Statement: _______________________________

____

Chosen Pattern:

Centering Stone/meaning: ____________________________

First layer/meaning: ________________________________

Second layer/meaning: ______________________________

Third layer/meaning: _______________________________

Fourth layer/meaning: ______________________________

Parameter stones/meaning: ___________________________

Additional accessories: _____________________________

Healing modalities to include: ________________________

____

____

Observations/Signs:

____

____

____

____

____

____

Reflections and Insights...

CHAPTER NINE - Execution - remote gridwork missions

More and more, people are feeling very called to participate in group gridworker missions virtually. This provides much greater access to both the magnifying power of shared intentions as well as shared psychic gifts, but also unlimited access to locations that would be otherwise impossible to travel to. There are many established remote gridworking groups that can be found online, and each group has its own special flow that has been created and perfected by the individual gridwork facilitator. This chapter is about remote gridwork missions from the perspective of a fledgeling gridwork facilitator.

Many of the basic principles here are the same as physical crystal gridworking, however there is a much greater emphasis on research, planning and ceremonial aspect. There does not need to be that physical anchor that a crystal provides in the location; the participants are doing the anchoring with their intentions. Although you may find that spontaneous work is quite effective, often spending the time to really study the area that you wish to target, as well as planning the mission to fall within the most beneficial time to take advantage of cosmic and planetary influences will yield the greatest manifestation.

Consider the differences between both types of gridwork missions and compare and contrast them. How do you resonate with each?

____

____

____

____

____

____

Drafting Your First Remote Mission -

Establish your Itinerary template, which you will share with your group before beginning the mission. It should flow smoothly, and contain all the elements that are needed for everyone to be fully prepared to take on their individual roles, and be clear on the process and the purpose of the steps. Once you create your template, you can use it as the basic foundation of future remote gridwork missions. To review a template for several actual remote missions, see appendix from *A Portal to Earth Energy.*

Step One: Determine your targeted location, and the purpose of the mission. What is it specifically that you intend to manifest?

- Example: Releasing tortured souls and healing land trauma from Salem Witch Trials, Salem, Massachusetts.
- Your Draft statement:

____

Step Two: Determine the optimal day and time of the mission. What are the cosmic influences that are happening around that time? Are there any particular influences that are affecting your target location which you want to clarify?

- Example: March 2023; Neptune has crossed into Pisces, shattering illusions, healing trauma and restoring Divine connections. Heading into Aries equinox with lineup of planets in Aries, signalling new beginnings and powerful forward movement.
- Your Draft statement:

____
____
____
____

Step Three: Who are the members of your group, and what special skills and gifts will they be bringing to the mission? As you consider what specific sites you plan to touch upon quantomly through remote viewing/meditation, what roles can you identify for your various group members to take on?

- Example: Max is a dowser; he reads runes and has dragon protection. He strongly connects to the Violet Flame. He will cast the runes at the landing sight after the group has gathered there. Ingie is an energy healer with tuning forks and singing bowls. She has a strong I AM presence and will guide the group through the remote viewing journey experience. She will add sound frequency healing at each target location.
- Your Draft statement:

____
____
____
____
____
____

Step Four: Build your Opening Declaration, which is a prayer of invocation for Divine protection, and a statement of your highest intentions. This will very likely remain the same for all your future remote missions, so put careful thought into creating the first powerful Declaration you can.

- Example: "Creator of All Beings, we come together in service and shared purpose to assist the land to heal, and release all inversions and trapped energies. We call upon the protection and guidance of the Divine Most High, we call upon our true ancestors and spirit guides, and upon the Archangels. We declare our intentions to bring

forth only the frequency of love and above, and consent only to
these consciousnesses in our shared container. And So It Is!"
- Your Draft statement:

____

____

____

____

____

Step Five: Craft your statement of Mission Activation, where you
specifically recognize the Earth's grid template, and the powerful
Creative force that runs through the planet. Each member of the mission
should speak their own intention to participate in the work of restoring
the land and running pure, organic frequency of Divine Source through
the planetary grid. This will also likely remain the same as you progress
through future missions.

- Example: "Connected, we stand together, and activate the Diamond
  Crystal core of Earth, the waters, the fires, and the winds through
  four cardinal directions; North, South, East and West. We call forth
  the pure plasma Founder Flames, and declare our intention to assist
  the Guardians to open the Star Gates and restore all inversions,
  healing and releasing trauma from the land, and assisting trapped
  souls to return to Source. We activate our merkabah, and speak the
  way forward."
- Your Draft statement:

____

____

____

____

____

____

____

Step Six: Craft a statement to call upon the spirit animals or magical creatures with whom your group members connect, to be present during the mission and give assistance and protection. Are there relationships with Wolf spirit, or sphynx, or dragon? Include these in your Request, which you will also use for future missions.

- Example: "We call upon the powerful archetypal energies of our brothers and sisters, the magical guardian creatures of the multiverse. Merfolk- holders of the ancient sisterhood power, Feline Familiars- warriors of independence and Sovereignty.....we ask that you surround us and bring forth your energies on behalf of the Earth's grid and all life to assist this mission."
- Your Draft statement:

____
____
____
____
____
____
____
____
____

Step Seven: Create an anchoring Prayer of Unity to be spoken during the mission any time the group needs a recalibration back to a place of shared focus and intention whenever division or disruptive energies targeting egos are detected during the work. This may or may not be included as part of the regular remote mission; you may choose to have it available at the beginning of your itinerary and call attention to it with the team members when you come together to begin the work. The same is true for the Fear Removal Declaration.

- Example: "Brothers and Sisters, fellow warriors in service to the Flames of Creation, the Earth and all organic life thereon, we are Soul Family from across all cosmic nations and dimensions, united here under one purpose. Renew now, remember and rededicate to the shared mission. I avow my dedication to our sacred, shared purpose and do not consent to any artificial and inorganic intentions; I release all incoherence back to Source! And So It Is."
- Your Draft statement:

____

____

____

____

____

____

____

____

Step Eight: Create a fear removal Prayer to be spoken during the mission any time that anyone feels the need for focused protection, or when someone detects entities attempting to influence or attack the group, or any one member.

- Example: "I invoke the protection of the Diamond Crystal Light of Source and call upon the Divine Most High! Fill this Sacred Space with the pure Source consciousness, transmuting all fear and releasing it! I ask that my Teams focus on their spiritual, mental, etheric and emotional energy bodies and infuse with pure Source consciousness, releasing all fear-based and artificial programs and transmuting back to the light. And So It Is!"

Step Nine: Identify the specific locations that you will be targeting during the mission for clearing, healing and restoring. This is where you will spend the most time preparing, as this segment of the mission is where the focused work will be done. Often, you will discover that when you begin researching a landmark that is connected to a particular area, the search expands outward and you find other specific landmarks that are also connected. As you decide upon each landmark, plot its location on a map so that during the mission, members will be able to have visual cues to help focus their attention. Plug the target sites into your itinerary, and detail the work that will be done here with as much specificity as you can. Identify which member of the team will lead the group, reading through the itinerary at each location.

- Example: (from Mission to Salem) "Howard Street Cemetary - Giles Corey's execution and burial/haunting; Asking for Divine intervention and assistance to collapse portals, seal off implant technologies, and channel the organic Krystos frequencies back into the Earth's grid, cleansing and healing the ground with the White Flame of Purification, releasing all trapped soul fragments back to Source with recognition of their highest Divine purpose! (Speak Ho'oponopono together as a group) PORTAL IS CLOSED."
- Your Draft statement:

____

____

____

____

____

____

____

____

____

Step Ten: Identify your landing site, and your extrication site for the mission. These must be protected, safe places of power where infiltration and hijacking from outside forces are unlikely to be attempted. When the group begins the guided remote viewing journey, the landing site is where you will all initially arrive at, before moving to each specific target location.

- Example: In Mission to Boston, my group used Marblehead Lighthouse as both our landing and extrication sites. I chose this because I have a strong connection to and resonance with it. I visited this site in the past, communed with and anchored it energetically. I also carry a piece of it with me in photos, so the connection is continuously fed and renewed.
- Your draft statement:

____
____
____
____
____
____

Step Eleven: Add in any additions that you feel called to include during the mission. This may be a specific intention for this individual mission, and will not be included in future missions, or it may be something that you keep.

- Example: One of my team members was asked to create a special prayer for a mutual friend who is going through emotional trauma, persecution and heartbreak. She led us all in prayer for this friend when we arrived at our landing site at the lighthouse.
- Your Draft statement:

____
____
____

Step Twelve: Pull it all together into one smooth, flowing-format itinerary which is broken down into several segments, including preliminary recommendations (team members should prepare before joining, being sure to ground and shield and to charge their personal crystals), Zoom or virtual meeting room etiquette, and any other relevant additions. Be sure to include a final prayer/benediction at the end of the remote journey that will allow all the team members to focus and visualize the results of the work manifesting.

Remote gridwork mission itinerary templates are found at the end of this chapter for your use; develop and expand upon in whatever way works best for you and your work. You will also find more ideas and other examples available through research in books and on the internet. www.Indigoangel222.com (Amanda DiMarco) was a very valuable source of inspiration and wisdom for me as I began my journey of exploration into gridworking. Her guided gridwork journeys provided me with my initial template, that I took and made my own, and I acknowledge her with much gratitude and appreciation.

Reflections and Insights.....

____

____

____

____

____

____

____

____

____

____

____

Reflections and Insights...

ITINERARY - Remote Gridworker Mission

Title/Purpose : ____

____

Date/Time: __________________

Influences (local/cosmic):

____
____
____
____
____
____
____
____
____
____

Team Members- specialties & roles, tools, correspondences:

____
____
____
____
____
____
____
____
____
____

Landing and Extrication Sites for mission:

____
____
____

Housekeeping -   Zoom Etiquette/debrief instructions

____

____

____

____

Spiritual Hygiene -   Recommended prep work for members

____

____

____

____

PROTECTIONS -   Unity Prayer and Fear Removal Declaration

Unity Prayer:

____

____

____

____

____

____

____

____

Fear Removal Declaration:

____

____

____

____

____

____

____

MISSION

Opening Prayer/Declaration (by: _______________) -

____

____

____

____

____

____

____

____

Activation of Mission (by: _______________) -

____

____

____

____

____

____

____

____

Identification of Members/declaration of ceremonial tools & psychic gifts:

____

____

____

____

____

____

____

____

MISSION (Page 2)

Call to Spirit Animals/Magical Creatures (by: ________________) -

REMOTE VIEWING - Guided journey to Landing Site (by: ____________)

Guided Journey -Targeted Locations/guided Work (by: ______________)

Targeted locations/work (cont'd..)

____

____

____

____

____

____

____

____

____

____

____

____

____

____

____

____

Guided Journey to Extrication Site/ Benediction & Close (by: ______________)

____

____

____

____

Debrief:

____

____

____

____

____

____

____

ITINERARY - Remote Gridworker Mission

Title/Purpose : ____

____

Date/Time: ____________________

Influences (local/cosmic):

____

____

____

____

____

____

____

____

Team Members- specialties & roles, tools, correspondences:

____

____

____

____

____

____

____

____

Landing and Extrication Sites for mission:

____

____

____

Housekeeping -   Zoom Etiquette/debrief instructions

____
____
____
____

Spiritual Hygiene -   Recommended prep work for members

____
____
____
____

PROTECTIONS -   Unity Prayer and Fear Removal Declaration

Unity Prayer:

____
____
____
____
____
____
____
____

Fear Removal Declaration:

____
____
____
____
____
____
____
____

MISSION

Opening Prayer/Declaration (by: _______________) -

____
____
____
____
____
____
____

Activation of Mission (by: _______________) -

____
____
____
____
____
____
____

Identification of Members/declaration of ceremonial tools & psychic gifts:

____
____
____
____
____
____
____
____

Call to Spirit Animals/Magical Creatures (by: ______________) -

____
____
____
____
____
____
____
____
____

REMOTE VIEWING - Guided journey to Landing Site (by: ______________)

____
____
____
____
____
____
____

Guided Journey -Targeted Locations/guided Work (by: ______________)

____
____
____
____
____
____
____
____
____
____
____

Targeted locations/work (cont'd..)

____

____

____

____

____

____

____

____

____

____

____

____

____

____

Guided Journey to Extrication Site/ Benediction & Close (by: ______________)

____

____

____

____

Debrief:

____

____

____

____

____

____

ITINERARY - Remote Gridworker Mission

Title/Purpose : ____
____

Date/Time: ____________________

Influences (local/cosmic):

____
____
____
____
____
____
____
____
____
____

Team Members- specialties & roles, tools, correspondences:

____
____
____
____
____
____
____
____
____
____

Landing and Extrication Sites for mission:

____
____
____

Housekeeping -   Zoom Etiquette/debrief instructions

____

____

____

____

Spiritual Hygiene -   Recommended prep work for members

____

____

____

____

PROTECTIONS -   Unity Prayer and Fear Removal Declaration

Unity Prayer:

____

____

____

____

____

____

____

Fear Removal Declaration:

____

____

____

____

____

____

____

MISSION

Opening Prayer/Declaration (by: _______________) -

____
____
____
____
____
____
____
____

Activation of Mission (by: _______________) -

____
____
____
____
____
____
____
____
____

Identification of Members/declaration of ceremonial tools & psychic gifts:

____
____
____
____
____
____
____
____
____

MISSION (Page 2)

Call to Spirit Animals/Magical Creatures (by: _______________) -

____

____

____

____

____

____

____

REMOTE VIEWING - Guided journey to Landing Site (by: _______________)

____

____

____

____

____

Guided Journey -Targeted Locations/guided Work (by: _______________)

____

____

____

____

____

____

____

____

____

____

____

MISSION (Page 3) -

Targeted locations/work (cont'd..)

____

____

____

____

____

____

____

____

____

____

____

____

____

____

____

____

Guided Journey to Extrication Site/ Benediction & Close (by: _____________)

____

____

____

____

Debrief:

____

____

____

____

____

____

ITINERARY - Remote Gridworker Mission

Title/Purpose : ____

____

Date/Time: _____________________

Influences (local/cosmic):

____

____

____

____

____

____

____

____

Team Members- specialties & roles, tools, correspondences:

____

____

____

____

____

____

____

____

____

Landing and Extrication Sites for mission:

____

____

____

Housekeeping -   Zoom Etiquette/debrief instructions

____
____
____
____

Spiritual Hygiene -   Recommended prep work for members

____
____
____
____

PROTECTIONS - Unity Prayer and Fear Removal Declaration

Unity Prayer:

____
____
____
____
____
____
____
____

Fear Removal Declaration:

____
____
____
____
____
____
____

MISSION

Opening Prayer/Declaration (by: ______________) -

____
____
____
____
____
____
____

Activation of Mission (by: ______________) -

____
____
____
____
____
____
____

Identification of Members/declaration of ceremonial tools & psychic gifts:

____
____
____
____
____
____
____

MISSION (Page 2)

Call to Spirit Animals/Magical Creatures (by: _______________) -

____

____

____

____

____

____

____

REMOTE VIEWING - Guided journey to Landing Site (by: _______________)

____

____

____

____

____

Guided Journey -Targeted Locations/guided Work (by: _______________)

____

____

____

____

____

____

____

____

____

____

Targeted locations/work (cont'd..)

____
____
____
____
____
____
____
____
____
____
____
____
____
____

Guided Journey to Extrication Site/ Benediction & Close (by: _____________)

____
____
____
____

Debrief:

____
____
____
____
____

ITINERARY - Remote Gridworker Mission

Title/Purpose : ____

____

Date/Time: ____________________

Influences (local/cosmic):

____
____
____
____
____
____
____
____
____
____

Team Members- specialties & roles, tools, correspondences:

____
____
____
____
____
____
____
____
____
____

Landing and Extrication Sites for mission:

____
____
____

Housekeeping -   Zoom Etiquette/debrief instructions

____

____

____

____

Spiritual Hygiene -   Recommended prep work for members

____

____

____

PROTECTIONS -   Unity Prayer and Fear Removal Declaration

Unity Prayer:

____

____

____

____

____

____

____

____

Fear Removal Declaration:

____

____

____

____

____

____

____

MISSION

Opening Prayer/Declaration (by: _______________) -

____
____
____
____
____
____
____
____

Activation of Mission (by: _______________) -

____
____
____
____
____
____
____
____
____

Identification of Members/declaration of ceremonial tools & psychic gifts:

____
____
____
____
____
____
____
____

MISSION (Page 2)

Call to Spirit Animals/Magical Creatures (by: _______________) -

____

____

____

____

____

____

____

REMOTE VIEWING - Guided journey to Landing Site (by: _____________)

____

____

____

____

____

____

Guided Journey -Targeted Locations/guided Work (by: _____________)

____

____

____

____

____

____

____

____

____

____

Targeted locations/work (cont'd..)

____

____

____

____

____

____

____

____

____

____

____

____

____

____

____

____

Guided Journey to Extrication Site/ Benediction & Close (by: _______________)

____

____

____

____

Debrief:

____

____

____

____

____

____

ITINERARY - Remote Gridworker Mission

Title/Purpose : _______________________________________

____

Date/Time: ___________________

Influences (local/cosmic):

____
____
____
____
____
____
____
____

Team Members- specialties & roles, tools, correspondences:

____
____
____
____
____
____
____

Landing and Extrication Sites for mission:

____
____
____

Housekeeping -   Zoom Etiquette/debrief instructions

____
____
____
____

Spiritual Hygiene -   Recommended prep work for members

____
____
____
____

PROTECTIONS -   Unity Prayer and Fear Removal Declaration

Unity Prayer:

____
____
____
____
____
____
____
____

Fear Removal Declaration:

____
____
____
____
____
____
____
____

MISSION

Opening Prayer/Declaration (by: _______________) -

____

____

____

____

____

____

____

Activation of Mission (by: _______________) -

____

____

____

____

____

____

____

Identification of Members/declaration of ceremonial tools & psychic gifts:

____

____

____

____

____

____

____

Call to Spirit Animals/Magical Creatures (by: _______________) -

____

____

____

____

____

____

____

____

REMOTE VIEWING - Guided journey to Landing Site (by: _____________)

____

____

____

____

____

____

Guided Journey -Targeted Locations/guided Work (by: _____________)

____

____

____

____

____

____

____

____

____

Targeted locations/work (cont'd..)

____

____

____

____

____

____

____

____

____

____

____

____

Guided Journey to Extrication Site/ Benediction & Close (by: ______________)

____

____

____

Debrief:

____

____

____

____

____

ITINERARY - Remote Gridworker Mission

Title/Purpose : _______________________________________

____

Date/Time: _____________________

Influences (local/cosmic):

____
____
____
____
____
____
____
____
____
____

Team Members- specialties & roles, tools, correspondences:

____
____
____
____
____
____
____
____
____

Landing and Extrication Sites for mission:

____
____
____

Housekeeping -   Zoom Etiquette/debrief instructions

____
____
____
____

Spiritual Hygiene -   Recommended prep work for members

____
____
____
____

PROTECTIONS -   Unity Prayer and Fear Removal Declaration

Unity Prayer:

____
____
____
____
____
____
____
____

Fear Removal Declaration:

____
____
____
____
____
____
____

Opening Prayer/Declaration (by: _______________) -

____

____

____

____

____

____

____

____

Activation of Mission (by: _______________) -

____

____

____

____

____

____

____

____

Identification of Members/declaration of ceremonial tools & psychic gifts:

____

____

____

____

____

____

____

____

____

MISSION (Page 2)

Call to Spirit Animals/Magical Creatures (by: _______________) -

____

____

____

____

____

____

____

REMOTE VIEWING - Guided journey to Landing Site (by: _____________)

____

____

____

____

____

Guided Journey -Targeted Locations/guided Work (by: _____________)

____

____

____

____

____

____

____

____

____

Targeted locations/work (cont'd..)

____

____

____

____

____

____

____

____

____

____

____

____

____

____

Guided Journey to Extrication Site/ Benediction & Close (by: _______________)

____

____

____

____

Debrief:

____

____

____

____

____

____

ITINERARY - Remote Gridworker Mission

Title/Purpose : ____

____

Date/Time: ____________________

Influences (local/cosmic):

____

____

____

____

____

____

____

____

Team Members- specialties & roles, tools, correspondences:

____

____

____

____

____

____

____

____

Landing and Extrication Sites for mission:

____

____

____

Housekeeping -   Zoom Etiquette/debrief instructions

____
____
____
____

Spiritual Hygiene -   Recommended prep work for members

____
____
____
____

PROTECTIONS - Unity Prayer and Fear Removal Declaration

Unity Prayer:

____
____
____
____
____
____
____
____

Fear Removal Declaration:

____
____
____
____
____
____
____
____

MISSION

Opening Prayer/Declaration (by: _______________) -

____

____

____

____

____

____

____

Activation of Mission (by: _______________) -

____

____

____

____

____

____

____

Identification of Members/declaration of ceremonial tools & psychic gifts:

____

____

____

____

____

____

____

MISSION (Page 2)
Call to Spirit Animals/Magical Creatures (by: _______________) -

REMOTE VIEWING - Guided journey to Landing Site (by: _____________)

Guided Journey -Targeted Locations/guided Work (by: _______________)

Targeted locations/work (cont'd..)

____
____
____
____
____
____
____
____
____
____
____
____

Guided Journey to Extrication Site/ Benediction & Close (by: _____________)

____
____
____
____

Debrief:

____
____
____
____
____
____
____

A Final Word on the Cold False Light; A "New Age" Trap

The spiritual purpose of a "trigger" is to hold up a mirror and show places where people need to heal and grow.....to alchemize. When a trigger is faced head-on and transformed rather than just allowed to pull someone into a programming loop of reaction, cathartic healing can take place, and consciousness rises. This chapter will trigger many people, and you are encouraged to explore the information presented here from a well-grounded internal place.

All the mainstream systems have been created to "assist" humanity in theory, but in practice all serve as a mechanism of thought control through programming and enforcement by an illusion of consensus. It is an illusion because it is well-known by truly awake people that what lies behind the appearance is actually an anti-life consciousness that must enslave in order to feed upon the life-force of others. Anti-life consciousness is by definition disconnected from Source, which is the only true origin of life force energy. In a reality where the baseline consciousness of all beings who exist there is at love (500 frequency on the scale of consciousness) or above, true freedom exists organically. Freedom and love are of the same frequency, and this is the place where the high heart activates, where there is mutual recognition of the Divinity of all beings, and no need....or desire......for control or manipulation. It is a place of pure Sovereignty, where beings live in one-ness and in service to others, and in service to truth spontaneously, free of all coercion.

If you haven't heard of the Scale of Consciousness (Source: David R. Hawkins *Power Versus Force*) do a quick internet search and review the topic. What are your thoughts on it? How can you apply the principles to your own life?

____

____

____

____

____

____

____

____

____

Service-to-self consciousness is very rampant upon the Earth, and has been for many generations. The devolution of societies away from core connection to Earth, family and community into dead-zones of cities, institutions and corporations has been ongoing with steady progression throughout the 1900s and is now a snowball of epic proportions. The Universal Law of Correspondence....As Above, So Below; As Within, As Without applies here; the degradations that are on display (for instance, chronic illness and addictions, loneliness and disconnection from neighbors/communities/family, inability to be one's authentic self, difficulty forming bonds and being in loving relationships, for example) are the result of what is happening in the Unseen Realms; they are actual evidence of the intentions and ongoing manipulations by lower-density consciousness entities behind the curtain.

What are some of the outer expressions which evidence this truth that come immediately to mind?

____

____

____

____

____

____

____

Organized religion is one such control system, and it is powerful in that it is exceptionally successful in its utilization of principles of cult mind control to keep people contained within little boxes, worshipping something "out there" and giving away personal power through a focus on someone else's teachings as ultimate truth. Putting all trust and belief in any written script, which is subject to corruption and manipulation in addition to the built-in issues with translation, is only possible through a complete lack of discernment and giving away personal power. And so, many aware, heart-connected, empathic people have rejected the traditional, and have been drawn into the so-called "New Age", because it is much more empowering in its acceptance of the unseen realms and emphasizes psychic abilities and personal experiences of these realms.

However, the New Age is even more dangerous territory than traditional religion, because of the very openness of its adherents to the consciousnesses that inhabit the unseen realms, who are just waiting to ensnare the unsuspecting. Many of these dark-consciousness entities are fallen angelics and soporic beings which originated as thought-forms within the fabric of the Multiverse. These cold false-light teachers and teachings have been very successful down through the ages in their tactics, and many people with the capacity to become highly evolved spiritually end up voluntarily enabling and even sometimes channelling parasitic entities. At best, this sends people down rabbit holes giving their power, time and life energy away worshipping something rather than spending time going within and truly working on self-growth, and at worst, engaging in practices that give manifestation energy to dark consciousness intentions. Sometimes, it even opens people up for actual possession. Again, this is the opposite of Sovereignty. No practice that encourages worship, that preaches being in denial of the actual existance of regressive consciousness entities, or which minimizes the importance of the physical vessel (the body) should be accepted at face value without objective observation, research and deep contemplation.

What has been your own experience, either within traditional religion, or the New Age?

____
____
____
____
____
____
____

What steps can you take to ensure that your discernment remains strong and your awareness focused?

____
____
____
____
____
____
____

The issue of discernment and false-light teachings is particularly applicable to gridworking, as patterns are ultimately based upon numbers and geometries. The fundamental principles behind the choice of certain patterns are elemental to ensuring that the work is done within the original organic templating and is Source-connected and sustainable, rather than being of finite-life.

An example of this is a system that has been popularized in recent years by mainstream influencers; Kabbalah. This system is based upon ten pillars/spheres....and is incomplete. It is tied to the finite-life, binary code system....which is an inorganic template that has been artificially overlaid upon Earth and has held the collective consciousness of the planet locked down in a frequency fence for aeons. These teachings are the origination of the finite-life daisy of death pattern that has been misnamed "the flower of life", with a geometry that reduces through decimals and is not Source-fed. They are connected to the Emerald Tablets of Thoth, rather than the Emerald Covenant of the Founders.

Take a moment and do an internet search for daisy of death and flower of eternal life patterns, and sketch them out. Do you see the difference in the structure and the angles of the patterns?

Everything that exists must be replenished, otherwise it will quickly decay and die. If Divine Source is not doing the replenishing, sustainence must come from some other life force; from parasitism. Mathematics reveals true origin, and this is where the old saying "numbers do not lie" actually stems from. The Earth's original Divine Source blueprint contains the sacred numbers three, six and nine; and can be confirmed through the study of Vortex Mathematics. It is highly recommended that you follow up with expansive study on the topic. A good place to start are the Trivium, the Quadrivium, the Cosmic, Natural Laws (or Principles) and Vortex Mathematics.

Reflections and Insights...

Reflections and Insights...

Other Books by the Author-

Crystal Grid Fairies Mission Series:
Mission Activated,Answering the Call of the Lighthouse
coming soon:
Mission to Heal Land Trauma from the Salem Witch Trials
Mission to Boston Restoring the Spirit of 1776

Crystal Grid Fairies Guide Series:
A Young Lightworkers Guide to Crystals and Consciousness
coming soon:
A Young Lightworkers Guide to Earth Energy
Crystal Grid Fairies Workbook

A Portal to Earth Energy, The Path of the Gridworker

About:

Kenzie Rhodes is a Doctor of Divinity and metaphysical practitioner who lives in Western Massachusetts with her family, and her three little boars. Yes, Anandi and his friends are real! She began working with Earth Energies after a series of unusual events alerted her to her true mission as a Gridworker, and a Gridwork Facilitator.
kayazuray@yahoo.com

www.crystalgridearthenergyhealing.com
The Crystal Grid Fairies series books were created to serve as a Lighthouse for young fairy lightworkers, who came here for a different reason.

CRYSTAL GRID FAIRIES WORKBOOK

Companion to
CRYSTAL GRID FAIRIES
Series for Young
Lightworkers

by Kenzie Ann Rhodes

Crystal Grid Fairies- A Young Lightworker's Mission and Guide Series
Published by Azuray Productions;
Hampden County on Massachusetts
Copyright © 2023 by Kenzie Rhodes

Azuray
Productions

Table of Contents

Introduction to the Workbook.......................4
Chapter One   ....

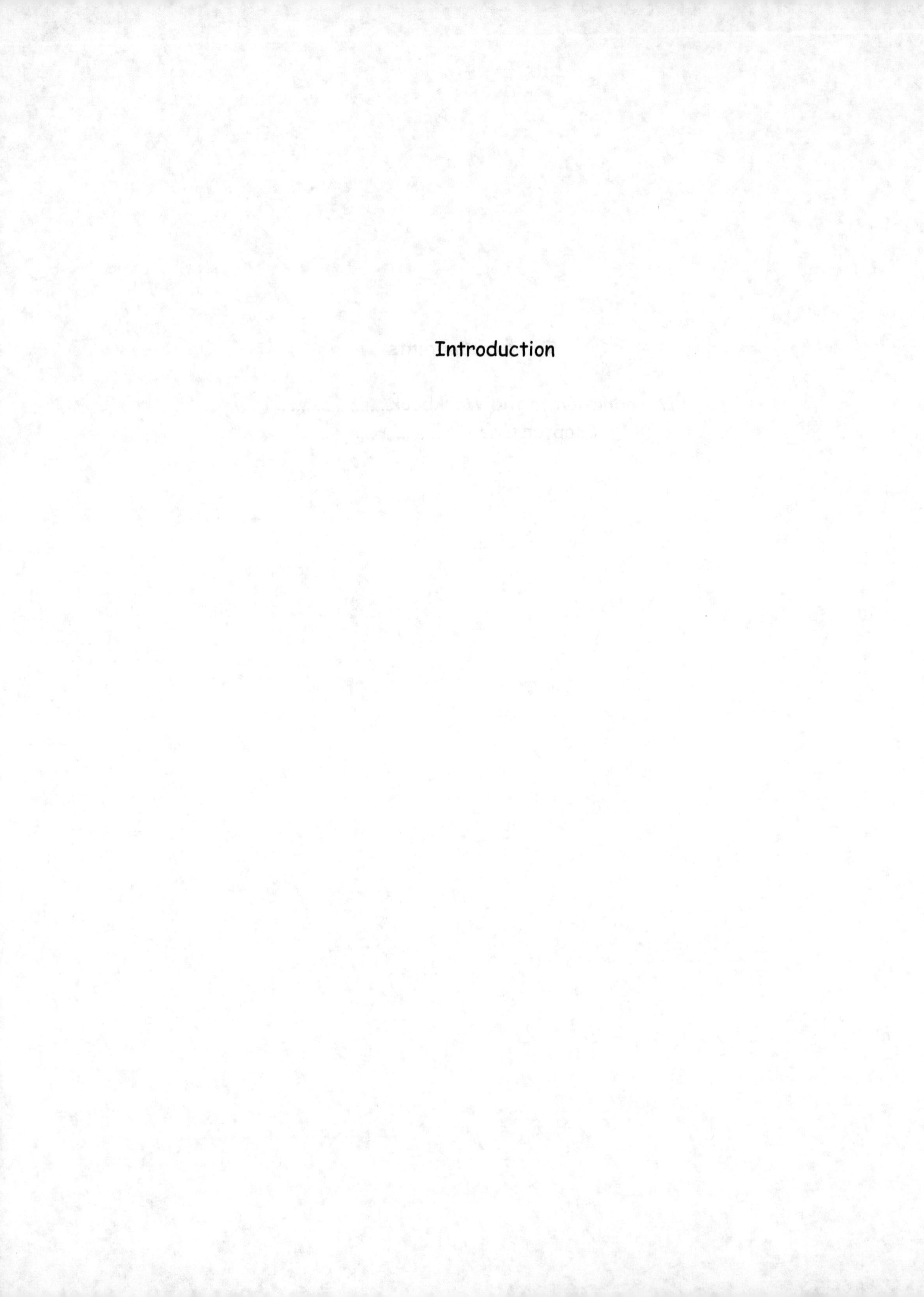

Introduction